For Dylan,
in memory of Taylor Marie Teut
—K. D.

Special thanks to Steve Malk,
who saw potential in a little sketch of a raccoon
—S. G.

atheneum
ATHENEUM BOOKS FOR YOUNG READERS
An imprint of Simon & Schuster Children's Publishing Division
1230 Avenue of the Americas, New York, New York 10020

For information about special discounts for bulk purchases, please contact
Simon & Schuster Special Sales at 1-866-506-1949 or business@simonandschuster.com.
The Simon & Schuster Speakers Bureau can bring authors to your live event.
For more information or to book an event, contact the Simon & Schuster Speakers Bureau
at 1-866-248-3049 or visit our website at www.simonspeakers.com.
Book design by Lauren Rille
The text for this book was set in Farnham.
The illustrations for this book were rendered in pencil and ink and then assembled and colored digitally.
Manufactured in China
0417 SCP
First Edition
10 9 8 7 6 5 4 3 2 1
Library of Congress Cataloging-in-Publication Data
Names: DiPucchio, Kelly, author. | Graegin, Stephanie, illustrator.
Title: Super Manny stands up! / by Kelly DiPucchio ; illustrated by Stephanie Graegin.
Description: First edition. | New York : Atheneum Books for Young Readers, [2017] | Summary:
"The story of a brave little raccoon named Manny, whose superhero games at home give him unexpected strength at school
when he puts on his invisible cape to stand up to a bully"—Provided by publisher.
Identifiers: LCCN 2015028659 | ISBN 9781481459600 (hardcover) | ISBN 9781481459617 (eBook)
Subjects: | CYAC: Raccoon—Fiction. | Imagination—Fiction. | Bullying—Fiction.
Classification: LCC PZ7.D6219 Su 2017 | DDC [E]—dc23
LC record available at http://lccn.loc.gov/2015028659

SUPER MANNY STANDS UP!

written by
KELLY DiPUCCHIO

illustrated by
STEPHANIE GRAEGIN

atheneum
Atheneum Books for Young Readers
New York London Toronto Sydney New Delhi

Every day Manny put on a different cape after school.

When he wore his blue cape, he saved the world from an ocean of unsavory sea creatures.

I AM FEARLESS!
SOAP

In his red cape, Manny battled an angry army of zombie bears.

ROAR!!
I AM STRONG!

He soared through the skies in his yellow cape

and single-handedly brought down the evil cloud monsters.

When legions of alien robots with laser-beam eyes invaded, Manny tirelessly fought them off in his purple cape.

I AM POWERFUL!

A green cape usually meant Manny was taking on the forest giants, defeating them one at a time.

Traveling to the far reaches of the galaxy to fight crime and injustice wasn't easy, but that's what superheroes do.

Manny always saved his *top secret undercover* cape for school.

With it, he battled mutant monkeys.

He stopped fiery comets heading straight for Earth.

He faced down giant squids with long tentacles and red eyes—

SAID MOVE!

Manny looked past
his lunch to see where
the loud voice was
coming from.

Tall One was towering over Small One and laughing.

“MOVE, little weirdo!” he said.

Small One seemed to get even smaller.

Manny watched as Tall One continued his laughing and teasing.

He felt frozen.
Glued to his seat.
So he said nothing.

He did nothing.

Until he remembered his invisible cape!

Manny stood up.
And then he did the bravest,
most courageous, kindest thing
he ever could have done. He said:

EAT YOUR GREENS!

Tall One moved in closer. *"What did you say?"*
Manny saw a storm of evil cloud monsters swirling around Tall One's head. But he had stared into the eyes of zombie bears, unsavory sea creatures, and forest giants before, so he didn't back down.

He reminded himself,

I AM FEARLESS.

I AM STRONG.

I AM BRAVE.

I AM POWERFUL.

I AM INVINCIBLE!

"I said STOP IT," he repeated,
a little louder this time. "You're being mean."

At that moment, everyone around him remembered they too were heroes with their own invisible capes.

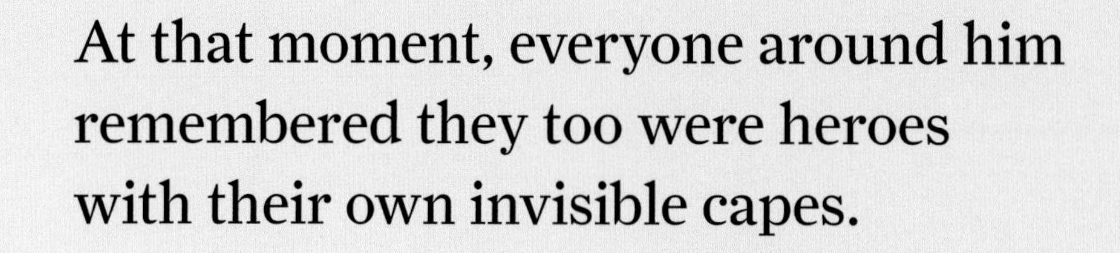

STOP IT.
That's not nice!
YEAH, STOP IT!
stop it.
EAT YOUR GREENS!

Tall One scowled. And then, just like the legions of alien robots with laser-beam eyes, he retreated.

Mission accomplished.

Small One was very grateful for the backup.

Manny was grateful too . . .

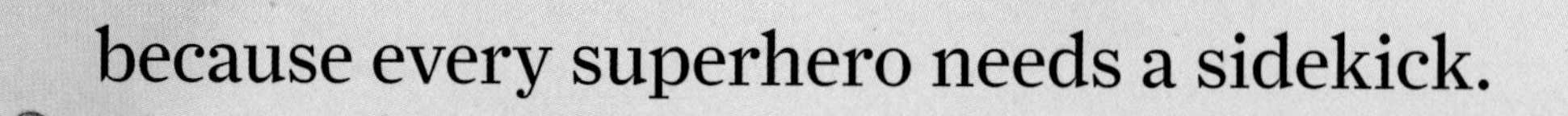
because every superhero needs a sidekick.